If You Find a Rock

PHOTOGRAPHS BY *Barbara Hirsch Lember*

If You Find a Rock

WRITTEN BY *Peggy Christian*

Houghton Mifflin Harcourt
Boston New York

www.hmhco.com

The Library of Congress has cataloged the hardcover edition as follows:
Christian, Peggy.
If you find a rock/written by Peggy Christian; photographs by Barbara Hirsch Lember.
p.   cm.
Summary: Celebrates the variety of rocks that can be found, including skipping rocks,
chalk rocks, and splashing rocks.
1. Rocks—Juvenile literature.   [1. Rocks.]   I. Lember, Barbara Hirsch, ill.   II. Title.
QE432.2.C478   2000
552—dc21   98-48938
ISBN 978-0-15-239339-7
ISBN 978-0-15-206354-2 pb

Manufactured in China
SCP 35 34 33 32 31 30 29 28 27
4500828912

The illustrations in this book are hand-tinted black-and-white photographs.
The display type was set in Opti Packard Bold.
The text type was set in Weiss.

If you find a rock,
a nice flat, rounded rock
that sits just right
in the crook of your finger,
then you have
a skipping rock.
You toss it out
in the water just so
and see it trip
across the surface,
making a chain
of spreading rings.

Maybe you find
a soft white rock—
a rock that feels dusty
in your fingers.
Then you have
a chalk rock,
and you use it
to make pictures
on the pavement.

Or you might find
a big mossy rock
by the side of
a long, steep trail.
Then you have
a resting rock,
and as you sit down
you feel
the cool moss
squush beneath you.

Then again,
you might find a rock
with a stripe running
all the way round it.
Trace the line
with your finger—
it must circle all the way.
You have
a wishing rock,
and you whisper
what you want
before you throw it.

If you find a rock—
a big rock—
by the edge of the water,
then you have found
a splashing rock.
When it hits the surface,
the water jumps
out of the way,
raining back down
on your outstretched hands.
The bigger the rock,
the wetter you get.

Maybe you find
a pile of small,
rounded pebbles.
Then you have found
sifting rocks,
and you can scoop up
a handful
and let them slide
slowly through
your fingers.

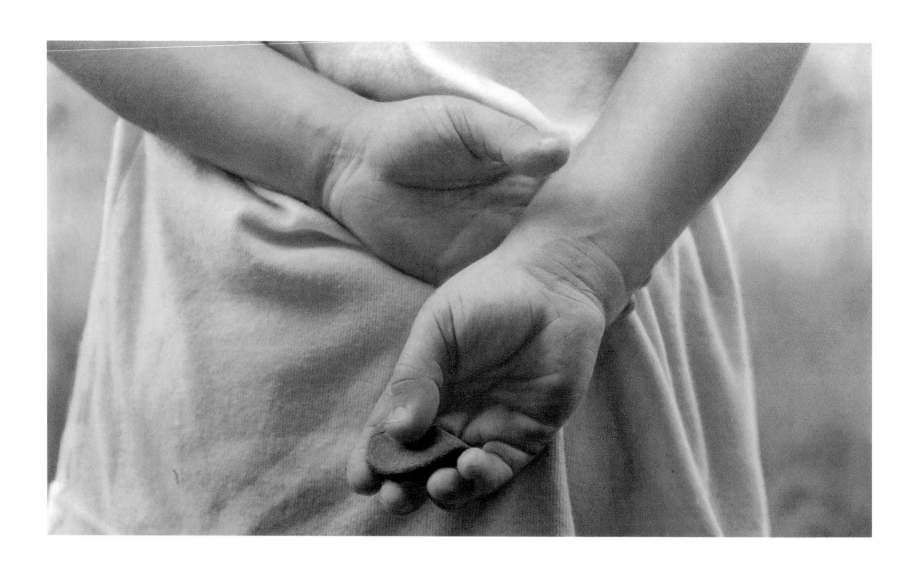

Or you might find a rock
whose water-smoothed surface
catches your eye.
If it feels easy
in your hand
when you rub it,
then you have found
a worry rock.
You rub it between
your fingers
and your troubles
are smoothed away.

Then again,
you might find a rock
sitting in a grassy field.
Push it over.
You have found
a hiding rock, and
in the cool, dark
underside live
all kinds of things
that creep and crawl and hide
out of sight.

If you find a rock—
a great rock—
that towers over you,
then you have found
a climbing rock.
Hold on with your toes and fingers,
grip hard as you
stretch up and pull
until you reach the top,
where you feel
much grander than you did
on the ground.

Maybe you will find
a twisting line of rocks
sticking up out of a creek.
Then you have found
crossing rocks,
which wait
to meet your feet
as you pass over
the water rushing away
all around you.

Or you might find
a rock with a print
of something else—
a leaf or a shell.
Then you have found
a fossil rock,
and you feel
the shape of something
that lived long, long ago
when the rock was young.

Then again,
you could find
a small, rounded rock
right in front
of your toe
as you go down
the sidewalk.
You have found
a walking rock,
and you kick it
ahead of you
and let it
lead you home.

If you find a rock—
a rock that's not
a skipping rock,
or a chalk rock,
or a resting rock,
or a wishing rock—
that's not
a splashing rock,
or a sifting rock,
or a worry rock,
or a hiding rock—
that's not even
a climbing rock,
or a crossing rock,
or a fossil rock,
or a walking rock,

but you like it anyway,
because it reminds you
of a place,
or a feeling,
or someone important—
then you have found
a memory rock,
and sometimes
those are the best
rocks of all.